JUST ANOTHER BUSY DAY

Written and illustrated by
Jacelen Deinema Pete

PEACHTREE PUBLISHERS, LTD.
ATLANTA

Published by
Peachtree Publishers, Ltd.
494 Armour Circle, NE
Atlanta, Georgia 30324

Manufactured in the United States of America

10 9 8 7 6 5 4 3 2 1

Design and illustration by Jacelen Deinema Pete

Library of Congress Cataloging-in-Publication Data

Pete, Jacelen Deinema, 1954-
    Just another busy day / Jacelen Deinema Pete.
        p. cm
    Summary: Three-year-old John enjoys a busy day of play as he drives his
  sports car (his tricycle), rides his horse (his hobbyhorse), and escapes into the
  world of his imagination.
ISBN 0-934601-93-3
[1. Play—Fiction. 2. Imagination—Fiction.]   I. Title
  PZ7.P44134Ju 1989   89-34825
[E]—dc20   CIP
                                                AC

Dedicated to John

and "Little Bear"

 **H**i. My name is John and I'm three. Some kids say, "There is nothing to do," but my day is always busy.

First, it's breakfast and then time to get
dressed to go outside. I am ready for anything.

There is my fast car to take for a drive.

r I can take my horse for a ride

at the rodeo.

Back in my yard, I find my baseball bat
and glove and hit a home run.

When I get hungry, I fix myself something to eat.

After lunch, Mom lets me play in the band, if I'm not too noisy.

But then comes "quiet time"
with my trains.

r I can paint a picture with my friends.

Sometimes I'm an acrobat, traveling with the circus.

I practice my golf swing in front of my fans.

After dinner, it's time for my bath . . .

with the fish, of course.

Then my busy day is done, except for my dreams. Tomorrow will be here soon.

Now,

who can say,

"There is nothing

to do"?

Freelance illustrator Jacelen Deinema Pete was born in Waverly, Iowa, and now makes her home in Kennesaw, Georgia. She graduated with a Bachelor of Arts degree from Colorado State University and is the mother of two sons. This is her debut children's book.